To Henry who endures
my difficult days, and vice versa

Kids Can Press Ltd. gratefully acknowledges the
assistance of the Canada Council and the
Ontario Arts Council in the production of this
book.

Canadian Cataloguing in Publication Data

Fernandes, Eugenie, 1943

A difficult day

ISBN 0-921103-17-4 (bound) ISBN 0-921103-80-8 (pbk.)

I. Title

PS8561.E76D53 1987 iC813'.54 C87-093546-1
PZ7.F47Di 1987

Book design by Michael Solomon
Printed in Hong Kong by Everbest

PA 89   0 9 8 7 6 5 4 3 2 1

A Difficult Day

Eugenie Fernandes

Kids Can Press • Toronto

Last night, Melinda couldn't sleep.
Crumpled sheets,
lumpy pillow,
crumbs in her bed...
it was awful!

In the morning, she couldn't wake up.
"Time to get up," said her mother.
"Hurry, you'll be late for school."

Melinda *was* late for school.
In gym class, stupid Harold punched her.
Melinda punched him back and they
both had to sit on the bench.

During recess, Melinda fell in a puddle.
She got filthy!
She didn't care.

At home, her mother told her to get in the tub.
Melinda didn't want to get in the tub.
"I don't care if I'm dirty," she said.
Her mother put her in the tub anyway.
Melinda complained, "You never listen!
You never listen! Nobody ever listens to me."

The water was nice and warm.
Melinda felt like a noodle

floating in a bowl of chicken soup.
It was good.

But good things never seem
to last long enough.
Her mother took her out of the tub.
"You look like a prune," she said.

"I *am* a prune," said Melinda.
"Leave me alone. I can dry myself.
Don't touch me! Don't touch me!"

Such talk made her mother angry.
Melinda, the prune,
was sent to her room.

She slammed the door.
"You can't come in.
Don't you try to come in," she said.
"I don't like you anymore.
I don't like anybody!"

Melinda grabbed her pillow
and hugged it tightly.
"Why don't you love me better?" she said.
Then she crawled underneath her bed.

09670

It was dark. Melinda felt
as if she were lost in space

and nobody even cared.

"I'm going away," she said.

"All the way to the other side
of the world."

"The people there will love me

and they'll hug me when I feel sad."

Meanwhile Melinda's mother was baking cookies.
She didn't feel angry anymore.
She felt sorry for Melinda.
"Poor thing. She's had a difficult day."

So her mother took milk and cookies
up to Melinda's room.

But Melinda was gone!

Her mother looked everywhere.
In the closet . . . behind the curtain . . .
in the attic.

She even looked in the laundry basket.
But she didn't find Melinda because
she didn't look under the bed.

"Mummy," said Melinda in a very little voice.
"Here I am. Do you still love me?"

"Do I love you?" asked her mother.
"I love you more than anything
in the whole world."
Then Melinda's mother crawled
under the bed, too.

She hugged and kissed her little girl.
Then she hugged and kissed her again.

"I was so scared when I couldn't find you,"
said her mother.
"Don't be scared," said Melinda,

"I love you too."

So after a difficult day,
Melinda and her mother
had milk and cookies,
underneath the bed.